Farmer Dillo
Paints His Barn

Jesse Adams

Pictures by Julie Speer
and Christopher Owen Davis

JOURNEY FORTH™

Greenville, South Carolina

S12622

Written by Jesse Adams
Illustration Concepts: Julie Speer
3D Illustrations: Christopher Owen Davis
Art Direction: Aaron Dickey
Additional 3D Support: Kenneth Bartlett, Jeffrey Sheldon & John Bjerk
Design: Chris Hartzler

© 2006 BJU Press
Greenville, SC 29614

Printed in the United States of America
ISBN 1-59166-481-0

15   14   13   12   11   10   9   8   7   6   5   4   3   2   1

To my nephew, Micah
-JA

To God, who blessed me
with the gift of drawing!
-JS

To my loving parents,
Solomon and Matilda Davis
-COD

Hello! This is Farmer Dillo.
He is the best farmer
in all of Sundown.

Farmer Dillo loves to work.
Yesterday he built a brand new
barn for his farm.

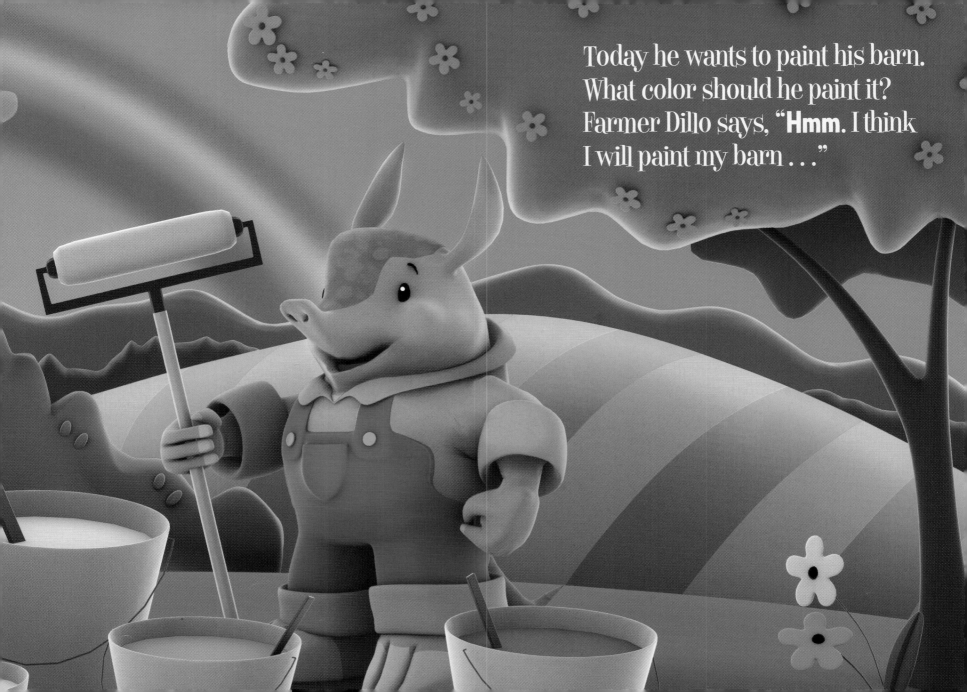

Today he wants to paint his barn. What color should he paint it? Farmer Dillo says, "**Hmm**. I think I will paint my barn . . ."

So, he does.

But when Farmer Dillo looks up at his blue barn, all he sees is the blue sky.

Can **you** find Farmer Dillo's barn?

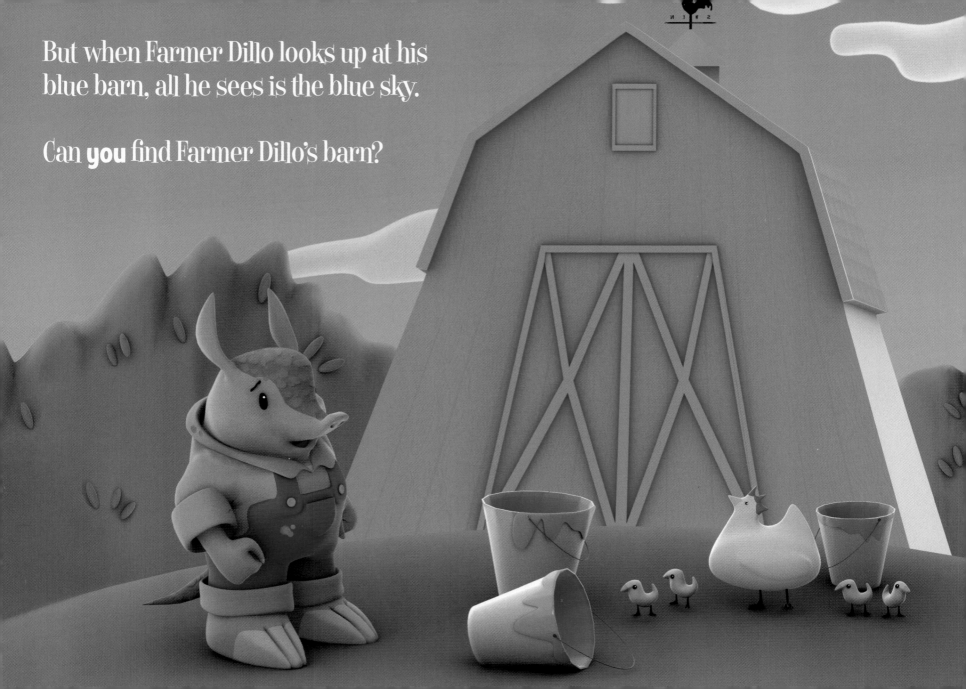

So Farmer Dillo says, "**Hmm.** My barn cannot be blue. I will paint my barn . . . **GREEN!**"

So, he does.

But when Farmer Dillo looks at his green barn, all he sees are the green trees.

Can **you** find Farmer Dillo's barn?

So Farmer Dillo says, "**Hmm.**
My barn cannot be blue.
My barn
cannot be
green.

I will paint my barn . . .
YELLOW!"

So, he does.

Power
Paint Pump

But when Farmer Dillo
looks up at his yellow barn,
all he sees is the yellow sun.

Can **you** find Farmer Dillo's barn?

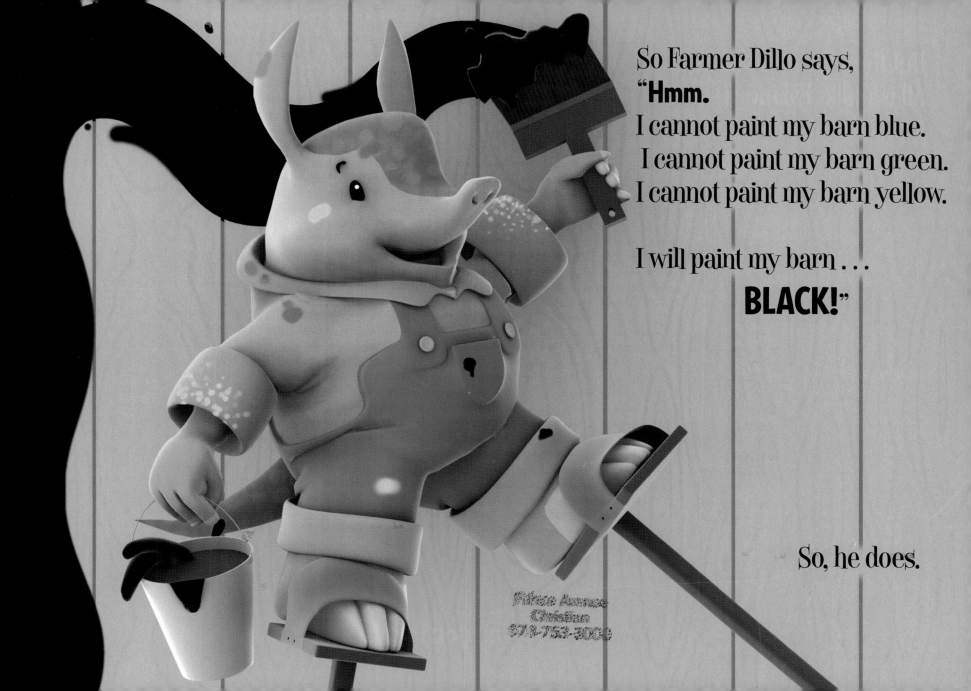

So Farmer Dillo says,
"**Hmm.**
I cannot paint my barn blue.
I cannot paint my barn green.
I cannot paint my barn yellow.

I will paint my barn . . .

BLACK!"

So, he does.

But then the sun sets and all is dark. Farmer Dillo looks for his black barn, but he can't find it in the dark.

Can **you** find Farmer Dillo's barn?

So Farmer Dillo says in the dark,
"Hmm.
I cannot paint my barn blue.
I cannot paint my barn green.
I cannot paint my barn yellow.
I cannot paint my barn black.

Tomorrow,
I will paint my barn . . ."

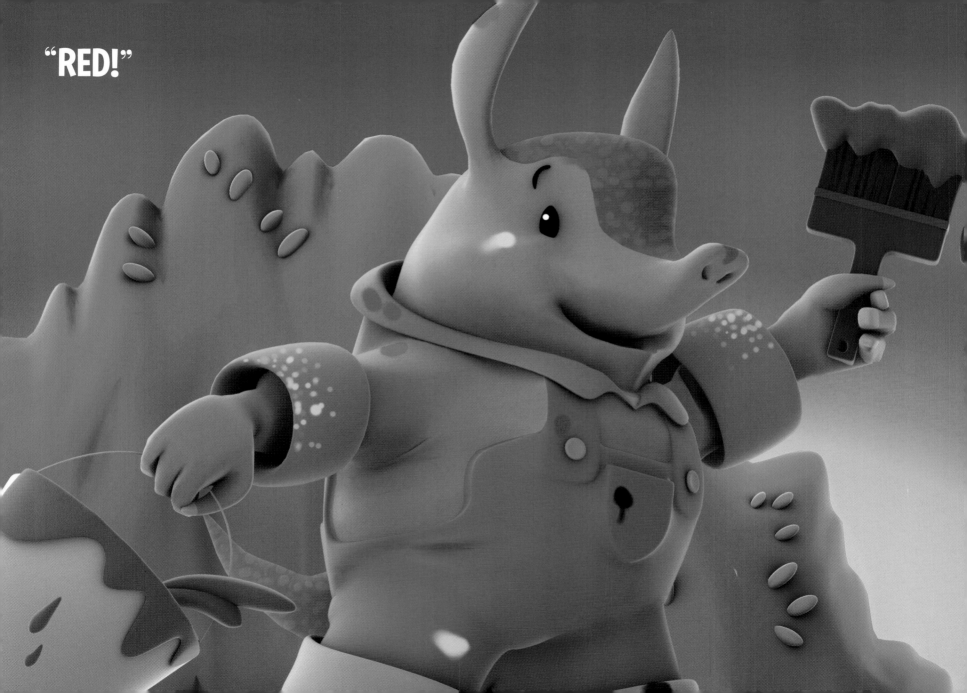

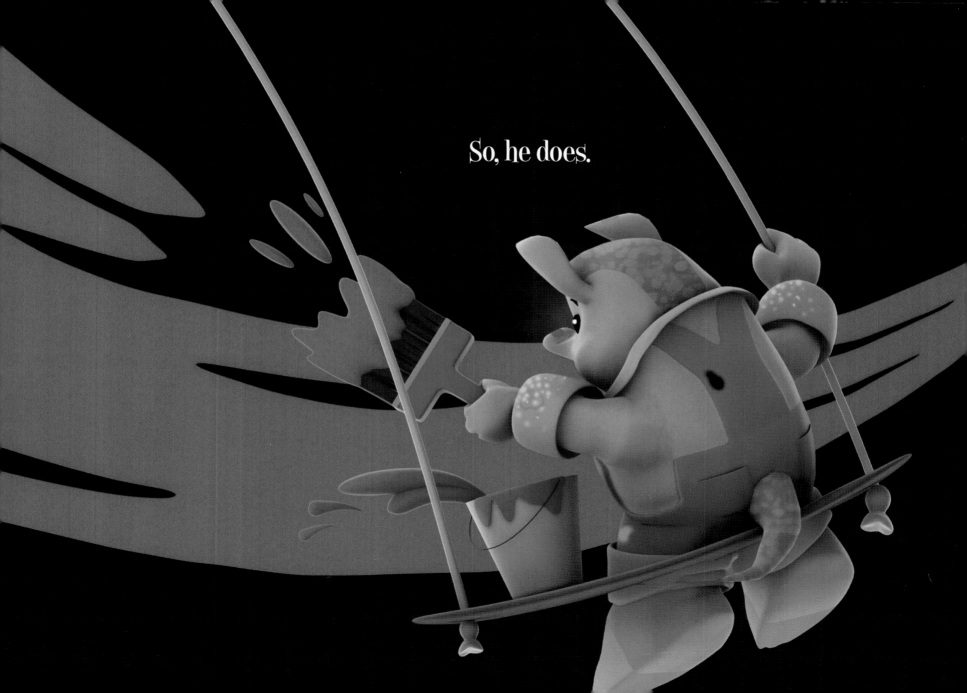

So, he does.

Farmer Dillo looks at his red barn.
He can see it in the blue sky.

Doesn't Farmer Dillo's red barn
look good in the blue sky?

Farmer Dillo looks at his
red barn by the green trees.

Doesn't Farmer Dillo's red barn
look good by the green trees?

Farmer Dillo looks at his red barn by the yellow sun.
Doesn't Farmer Dillo's red barn look good by the yellow sun?

Then the sun sets and all
is dark in Sundown.
Farmer Dillo looks at his
red barn in the dark.

He **STILL** can't see his red barn. But that's OK . . .

It's time for bed anyway.
Goodnight, Farmer Dillo!